FIRST MURDER

THIS IS NOT THE END, JUST THE BEGINNING

M. R. SHARVESHWAR

Contents

PREFACE

A Young girl, a stranger....

One laptop, one mobile...

One murder, one bad dream...

"WHETHER SHE WILL FIND HER"

When she came to know that she was used by him and Alexandra was playing in her life and she came to know on her birthday night.

She was wrong. She believed him and trusted him with all her life she didnt receive love instead she got only betrayal.

As she struggles to come out of her betrayal she also came to know about the fake websites which was used by Alexandra and her clients.

Whether she will be able to uncover them with an unknown stranger.

Acknowledgements

I firstly would like to thank my parents who allowed me to pursue my passion and what I wished from many years and all the team who worked in this book. Editors, Poetic Souls publishers who brought this book to the market and made me to achieve in my passion which I was dreaming.

INTRODUCTION

Sharveshwar spent his childhood in Kilkundah village , The Nilgiris, Tamil Nadu.He is from BADUGA community. Sharvesh is a graduate from the Adhiyamaan College of Engineering and satisfies his timing by reading and writting on his legible time. Now he is working in corporate and staying with his parents in Bangalore.

He found an id called "cutie_neha" and her bio read as "Love to speak with strangers" near to it was the red heart symbol and the next line has "DM boys" immediately he gave a request and sent a message

"Hi" and not even a single minute he got a reply.

.

"Hi" there was a mini smile in his lips then he replied back saying "Hru?"

.

He was the man who love to meet strangers and hookup and very desperate for sex as well and few seconds later reply came "I'm fine".

He was thinking like what to speak with her and how to hold a conversation.

Then another reply "U?"

Now he knows how to hold the conversation.

"I'm fine…Ur name?"

"Reshma… and urs?"

He doesn't want to tell his real name and replied back as "Rahul". Below his fake name there was "Seen". There was no reply for more than couple of minutes. He decided not to leave here and started typing.

"I'm frm bnglr and Ur from?"

"Same here".

"Your native is bnglr?"

"No...Im from Hubali"

"Oh kk..wru in bnglr...Area?"

"I'm not willing to reveal bc of my privacy"

He was mild disappointed on hookup now. Then he decided to reveal his thoughts now.

"I want to tell u something."

"Tell"

"I'm looking for sex...shall we have?". He thought of including "If ur interested" but then he is not going to give a chance.

There was a small red heart symbol below the text which means she liked the message and again a "Seen" but no reply. After a few minutes reply came.

"How much u can offer?"

"I can offer based on how u look....can I have a pic of urs?" within seconds she replied.

"No...not now."

Then he thought that only if someone ask for their pics, they will reply soon.

He was in the terrace, walking and seeing the sky like he finally found someone who can spend time and share his dark secrets which he was doing after he graduated from college.

"r u single?" he asked.

"Currently yes, had break up few months back." She replied

Then he decided not to leave her in any situation and in any moment.

"I'm looking for relationship as well." He said

There was a "Seen" and below the text "Tying...."

He was wondering what in the world she will reply and the reply came.

"U need sex r love?"

He was really confused now. If sex they can hookup and have nightstand that he was waiting for or love it will take years to have. In double minded he chooses "Love".

"r u sure?"

"I need sex not love."

"Tell clearly sex r love. If u need sex we can hookup and end everything in a single day... for relationship I need someone who really care abt me and understand me. I'm not ready for a relationship with sex right now. "

Again he looked the sky and now an eagle was flying near to his house. Watched the eagle and started walking from left to right side. Even he needed someone to share his feelings and what he had done for the past 2 years when he got the job. He felt more comfortable with her and decided to spend his time with her and started being active all the time in the Instagram. Not for his followers, not for his posts, likes and comments only for her.

Now he replied as "Love only love" again.

"U mean it?"

"Yes. I damn mean it"

There its started on that moment he felt something like there was someone for him now who really care him as a person and spend time with him and someone who trust him eventhough they did not meet and look at their eyes at all. He decided to be active all the time and reply in a micro seconds and make her comfortable all the time.

Now he ask "r u wrkng r studying?"

.

"wrkng"

.

"When can we meet?"

"U need love right..thn y ur asking this?"

"Do you think we can be in relationship for long time...without looking at each other?"

"If you really love me distance doesn't matter"

She is really cleaver and now he came to know that she is really good at hiding her privacy.

He doesn't know how to continue more and another text came "I wanna tell u something" within seconds he replied like he was really in love with her "wat?" and the text came which he was never expecting "I'm a BOY". He know she is started to play with him right now however he is not ready for playing he is in serious mode like when cat look at the mouse and he replied

"Stop playing" and there was a smiley at the end, smiley which closes both the eyes and laughing and she liked his message, a red heart. There was no text until he started texting again. He thought she is busy and asked "wat ur dng" and she replied as "Ntng" then he thought that why these girls like to send always late reply and make the boys to wait for them.

"I need to know more about you and I have more things to share with you..my dark secrets."

"Same here." She replied

Then he started wondering why these girls always reply with one word or two words reply. They doesn't have energy to type also.

"How many times u had sex before?" he asked

"7."

He got really shocked and he knows that only with her ex. When you are in a relationship count is nothing to worry about. Then he replied mentioning him as a virgin.

She texted back

.

"No GFs?"

.

"If I had a gf ...y will l be a virgin."

.

"Do u think I will have sex with some random guys?"

He got surprised with that question and he started thinking in a good and matured way, if a girl or a boy in a relationship why they will have sex with some random members. Then he replied "No...I think only with ur ex."

"Good"

Then he confirms that she loved him/ex with her heart and soul and then for some reason he left her or she.

"What r the languages u know?" he asked

.

"Eng, Hindi, Marathi and Kannada" she replied

.

"Staying alone r with family?" he asked

.

Then she replied "Na...with frnds". He doesn't know what is "Na" may be that is the stylish way of saying "No."

.

"u guys in a flat?"

"yes."

"BHK?"

"1".

Conversation got over when he sees a drop on his mobile screen and he looked up the sky which is black clouds and windy right now. He went down from the terrace and entered his home, which is an apartment with 2 floors and his home is in the 2nd floor.

He is working as Data Analyst in MNC Company which is 25- 30 km from his home. Now after getting promoted last month, now he got WFH option and currently he is working from home. He is staying in 1 BHK and his room with a double cot bed straight opposite to the door. Near to the door there is a table where, there is UPS connectivity to his PC and near to that there is a computer table which was brought by his uncle when he was 11 years old. There is few drawings in the table. On the left side there is a man with a dance pose with a hand on the floor and both the legs are in the air and the other hand on the head. He was really interested in drawings when he was in the high school. Drawings where done on the day of his public exams. It's like a stress buster to him after reading for the exams. Near to that there is an open cub board with 4 shelves. First shelf with some stationary items and few wrist watches. 2 were FastTrack. The latest one is a gift given by his "SANTA" on "SECRET SANTA" game which he played on his company before WFH and the other one which he bought on his birthday during his high school. There were couple of boxes with visiting cards which read "Kotak Mahindra Bank". His dad was working as an insurance agent before he got a job in sales and service company which is 5-6 km from his home. Few boxes like Titan wrist watch box, an apple earphone box and a pen stand and many pens inside it which is not writing.

On the second shelf there are 19 thriller and nail baiting books and he is a bibliophile, voracious reader, bookaholic and he is a craziest fan of author "James Patterson". In the 3rd shelf there are 4 bags with many documents like his and his parents mark sheets, his school group photos and much more. Then trimmer, hair dryer and an iron box. In the fourth shelf there is just a sewing machine named "SINGER." On the left of the cub board there is a closed dress cub board. His mom Poornima 43 year's old women, lost her 3 children's during her pregnancy and he was only left at last. Every mother are special but she is more than special to him because she grown him as a single mother for 8 years in a small village near to OOTY and her husband was working in HOSUR. She took care after him and her mother in law for 8 years by leaving her husband. He was in school and he is not matured enough and he doesn't know what was his age during that time when that horrible incident occurred in her life.

III

There were many neighbours around her house but he was really interested and keen on only with the grey paint house neighbour. Suresh and his wife Purnima and a daughter Yovisha. She was 6 and he was 11 and he usually speaks a lot with her compared to other neighbours. Purnima became close his mom after seeing their friendship. He was good at maths and he used to teach her maths and clear his doubts in addition, subtraction, multiplication and division. Her mom and dad helped her when she was sick and took her to doctor and they were like a good company to her. She and his mom became close to each other.

Trust was her big mistake. No one was in the house on that day except her mother in law. Suresh a man with clean shave like mid-thirties with broad shoulders and he is a government bus driver came into her house and tried to misbehave with her. She gave a slipper shot to that asshole and punched him at his face and he went to the ground. Suresh and his family were in rent with Nagul his owner.

She went directly to their owner and told the incident with brave and not with a single tears in her eyes. Nagul went with angry and kicked their front door and shattered everything out of their house and they cried and begged

"

him to stay in the same the place because they don't have any other place to stay but she never begged anyone and she did not even cry in front of them and stood like a judge who give order to the victims. She was not able to tolerate what happened to her and she had her pain with herself without telling his son who is not matured enough to understand. Then she told her husband this incident through phone call which he was not expected in his entire. He doesn't have a word to speak after hearing this shit. He did not think about anyone, he was only keen on his work and he was not able to ask a leave from his manager Prakash who is a jerk. He doesn't know what to do now he is 500km from this incident and he was not able to ask a leave.

He called his brother in law Sasi who is mid-twenties energetic doing horticulture flower business in Conoor. He is like another dad to her and when he heared this news he was in a full of rage with that monster and went to kill him or put a police complaint and arrest him. This news is also spread to her sister Sumathi. Sumathi and her husband Krishnan and their 2 sons Amrith and Tharachand aka Revanth came in a Xylo to see her. To protect her name and his son she said NO to her brother when he told regarding the police complaint and they left the village with cursing. They reached Coimbatore to her sister house and they were holding tightly hugging and cried at each other. Sasi, Krishnan, Sumathi, she and her son were sitting in a hall and spoke for entire night regarding this incident, she explained them everything like a candidate telling about him in a interview.

"There is no men in the house" Sasi said.

"When there is no men in the house then there is no protection in the house. Enough is enough, you are going to Hosur and from now on you are staying with your husband.

Call Sharan." Sasi said with full rage.

Sharan was studying 9th standard in Sister Alphonsa School that is a CBSE school near to their village. Average student with average marks. There is grade system in all the CBSE schools and he always get B grade that is 60-80 marks. After hearing his uncle scream he came out of the room and stood behind them. Everyone are looking at him and no words from their mouth.

"Look at him" Sasi said with pitiful voice.

"He doesn't know what fathers love is till now" everyone in the room nodded their heads.

"He should be with his father from now on and his education will be continued there. Get ready and pack your bags" he told to her sister.

"You and Sharan are moving to Hosur" he said.

IV

At 9PM they had dinner and locked their house everyone got ready and started their ride to Hosur and the driver was Krishnan. Sasi has an Alto before when his business was in the hike and pockets and wallets were filled with money. He has Alto for nearly 2 years and he that was more challenging to him when he need flower boxes to move from one place to another. Then he got a Mahindra truck to put the flower boxes for exporting. Even though he has these many vehicles but he did not learn driving. He tried to drive Alto once but he got confused with clutch and accelerator. He long pressed accelerator instead of clutch, Alto's left headlight got broken and front mirror got scratched and had an X shape in it. He left driving after the damage. Always he need someone for driving and that's the good thing to him because he will be always in his phone speaking with customers and he will not be able to concentrate on his roads and traffic and he doesn't want another headlight to be broken.

They reached Hosur by 6AM, he was sleeping in his mother lap. That is a priceless moment for everyone even you are big, matured or a married man with kids. He was blinking his eyes and he sees his uncle with his weapon speaking with someone. He looked up and his beautiful women in the world his mom was smiling at him and kissed his forehead. He smiled again and asked her "Where are we going?"

"We are going to see dad" she relied by hiding all the things happened to her and showed only a smile to him. Then he got up from her lap and sat up. He saw an auto before and Xylo was following. He sees someone got out from the auto with mid-thirties with salt and pepper hair style with pale white skin. Then he was walking towards the car and he was able to recognise that face and there was a smile in his face. He saw him after couple of years. That was his father Raju. His hero who taught him to ride cycle, who carried him on his shoulders from home and to the school.

"Hey. My boy" Raju said with energetic voice. He smiled back and got out from the car. His dad never kissed him always a smile and energetic words. He was really tired, he went directly to his dad room and slept on his bed. He doesn't know what happened after the rest of the time. Now its 1PM he came to conscious when he heard his mom was crying and speaking with someone in her phone. He doesn't know what is happening and he gently touched his mom and she wiped her tears, turned back and smiled at him.

"Why you are crying mom, with whom you are speaking?" he asked in a mournful voice.

She always hold her tears back and smiled at him and said "I was speaking with your dad and I miss him now, told him to come soon to see us" she said in a breaking voice and he knew that was a lie and he wants to know what is happening. There was a parcel near him and his mom opened and served lunch for him. After having lunch switched on the TV and started to watch cartoon and music channels and now her mom closed her eyes and went to sleep now.

He remember everything, everyone who made her life miserable and painful but she was a very bold women faced everything at the age of 28 and now she is in the bed watching her by sitting next to her. Same bold women now 48 years old sleeping next to him. He wants to hug her but he did not do that, kissed on her forehead and said "Love you mom" in a low voice.

He saw his grandmother photo next to him and stared on that picture for few minutes. She is the mother in law "Deviammal". She is one of the useless grandmother to him. He remember his mom words whenever she look at her photo, "She did not even touched you and carried you with love when your in childhood" and turned again to his mom and he thought in his mind "Really proud of you mom and for this asshole you left dad for 8 years and took care of her?" She was the only mother, only mother who left her husband for 8 years for only one reason, "Mother in law". She took care of her nicely and got a good name in the village and by neighbours but her mother in law was different.

Devi has 1.5 acres of land and cultivated properly by her husband Mathan. Mathan was really a honest and genuine person and everyone in the village has a huge respect towards him. When someone cross his house he will call them and have a few chit chat and serve them. He never left anyone in the village without giving food. He has a shop on the village and Raju his son started to take care of their shop at the age 13 and brought all the resources and stocks from Manjoor which is 5kms from their village. Manjoor its kind of small town where all the people in the village will go for their household things. Mathan even went to Delhi during 1800s and travelled everywhere and they had photographs on the wall. Even his photo was hanged on the wall which is quite big and that was a painting. He was dead before Sharan was born.

He always had a thought that Devi should have dead instead of Mathan because Devi is useless piece of shit to him.

V

He went to login. His fingers were on CTRL, ALT and DELETE. Typed his password and logged into the system but his mind was logged into Shreya. He took his phone again and the chat continues. She was online, but now few dirty chats.

"Please do share your number...I don't ask your pics and videos...

I just want to see your status and want to speak with u.. please"

"U can speak here(Instagram) with me."

"We can be sex partners if you are interested for life long."

"Life long??...There is no such things dera" and that's a typo from her.

"Heyy tats u in your profile?".

Now she replied as "No". He knows how to make others speak and he knows to hold the conversation.

"Ok...you are single right?"

She replied "Why??"

"I need u ..tats y...Ur busy?"

She was shocked by looking at his message and replied back "What?"

"Ya...see I'm looking forward to be with you...I'm damn serious...
are you serious with me...if your serious with me follow my profile."

"Sry I don't believe in such things."

"Im not joking..after lockdown first thing we can meet..u can have my word."

"Okay...Let's wait then."

"Okay...Let's wait then."

"Touch??...fine"

"Not only touch...."

"So u want sex?"

"Yup...are you chatting with someone?"

"Yes."

"Who's that" and his messages continues in a flow. He did not leave her. He want her badly.

"Who's that tell me
Are you busy?..can I text u later if you are busy
You seems to be busy

Then her reply came after 2 minutes "Somewhat yes"

"Follow my profile..catch you later."

She said ok and followed his profile as well.

He continued his office work and there was another message from her saying "Follow me dear." He smiled and ignored and continued his work.

After his work he locked the system and saw his mom, she is still in sleep. He left the room silently and went to terrace again.

He took his phone and started texting her again. "Hi...still you are busy??..late replies"

She replied "Hi"

"R u busy now?...please do reply..I'm waiting...from 6:30 I will be busy..I want to speak with u lot."

He waited for 10mins and lost his patience and started to text her again, chain of texts went from him.

Heyyy
wantedly you are doing this?

She was active but she was not replying. "I know ur there but not replying"

"Then shall I go?"

"I need to tell u something"

He did not leave her.Finally she replied him "Ohh dese"

"What is dese?"

Again a typo "*dear"

"What dress you are wearing now?"

"Dress? Why"

"No need pic...just tell me I want to imagine u"

"Ohh...Nothing a pant n a T shirt"

"Anyone with u now?

No reply from her for 2 minutes he lost his patience again and texted again "Are you there?...please do reply I want to tell u something"

"No I'm alone..tell me"

Then he told 3 words to her he meant it. Not only from lips from his heart.

"I Love you"

Then she replied back in seconds like she doesn't care "Okay"

"I mean it...I'm not joking r time passing."

Then she said "Is this what u that u wanted to tell"

"I have one more thing...I will be nude and I want to be with you in your room..will that happen?"

Again no reply. He texted again "You there?" no reply again" Bye I'm going" then her reply came "I'm there"

"I asked u something"

She said "no sorry". He did not felt bad instead he was trying to understand her feelings.

He asked "Why"

She replied "No nudes"

"I'm not asking pics" he said

"Yeah I know can't share my nude pics" she replied

He did not understand what she is trying to say. He is not interested in her nude pics. He texted again "You and me alone in a room...will that happen?"

There is a heart symbol below his message. She liked his message and now she understood what he was trying to convey.

"I know u r desperate to see me but still...let's see.." she replied

"No let's see and all...we need to meet each other ..we need to go to your flat on that day tell your friends to go out somewhere...u and me ..just you and me alone and much more."

She replied "Mmm"

.

"I'm really hairy body..you like hairs r do u want me to trim?"

.

She replied " Anything would be fine." Now he liked her message.

.

"Oh ho...u did not tell me your size..let me guess 34b?"

.

"Yaa..good at guessing the size...close to 34"

.

"I'm good at guessing and picturising" She liked now.

.

He then texted "Did anyone crushed that?

.

He sent a crying emoji. She asked "What?". He replied "Tats mine...34b is mine"

.

"Ur not my boyfriend". He replied "Can I be?"

.

Then he got a satisfied reply from her "Lets see"

VI

This was during his college 3rd year. They were in the 2BHK rent house in Hosur. He has his separate room .He was very lonely and he need some partner who should always chat and spend time with him. He decided to browse webcam websites to get a partner or to chat with someone. The main intention of him to find someone with dirty minded and get their personal information's and be in touch with them. He started to type as "Best webcam website" in browser. There are plenty of websites but nothing was satisfied for him. While browsing he came across a website called Chaturbate also known as "CR GIRLS". This website has many webcam models throughout the world. Immediately he signed up and created an account as "Mobby007". This name "Mobby" was inspired from the film "Step up" series that was the dance group name in that film called "Mob" and 007 is from the "James bond". His profile bio needs to be added every 24hrs it's not permanent. This website has a feature of broadcasting ourselves through integrated webcam present in the system/laptop. He started to create his profile with name as "Mobby 007" and added the details in the required fields. Country – India, Age- 21, there is a filter dropdown box to choose whether men, women, Trans genders to have access to his room. This website is international website has all the genders "MFGTL (Male, Female, Gay, Trans genders, Lesbian)" and he clicked on Women. Now only women's from all the countries have access to his room.

He has an all in one PC which has monitor, mouse and keyboard. CPU and speakers are inbuilt. Computer table which has few drawings in the left and right side. Those were drawn during his higher secondary board exams for his stress buster. On the left side was the HIPHOP dance pose where, left hand in the floor both the legs in the air and right in his head like saluting and he coloured the picture with black marker pen. Pose in the middle, left side of the picture was "HIP" written in crazy design and coloured with black and green markers. On the right side of the picture was "HOP". Near to picture right hand written "KEEP CALM" which was written diagonally in red marker and near to the right hand was "AND DANCE". In the keyboard puller he had drawn the dragon image says "NO MERCY". Now the dragon and the word "No" is completely disappeared only the other word "MERCY" is visible in light green .On the right side of the table was another dance pose where, both the legs were slight bend and left hand was stretched backwards and right hand is touching the cap and top of his drawing says "FREE STYLE" and the left side of the picture says "DANCE" and I the right side "REVOLUTION" which was written in the blue marker.

He did not leave the drawer also, in the top right corner of the table. He has drawn 2 images. 1st image is a man jumping in a freestyle, his both hands and legs where stretched like he doesn't care about anyone and about his future. 2nd image was again the upside down pose where both the legs were stretched wide in the air, body is in the curved posture, left hand in the ground and right touching the left leg. He has written "BREAK" above the stretched legs and below "The STREET" in diagonal. He locked his room, closed his room windows it was dark and now he switched on the lights. This website has thousands of members and will get separate room for the broadcasters. Broadcasters have options to mute the users, kick the users from their room if they behave in vulgar manner. Broadcasters can even promote their user to the "Moderator" based upon their activity in their room or if the broadcaster wish to. If the broadcaster become a webcam model of that website then there is a lot of things the user can do with the users and in their room.

The users is not only for watching the broadcaster, even they can chat with them but not with all the broadcaster. Few broadcaster can restrict the users with something called "Tokens". If the user has tokens then they are allowed to chat with the broadcaster otherwise the user message will not appear to the broadcaster. Users need to purchase tokens based upon their interest and token is not only for the chat purpose. Broadcaster has plenty of sex toys with them to make the user to turn on and engaged throughout their broadcasting. Every broadcaster has "Dildo" between their legs during their broadcast. If the user has token and the user sent tokens during the broadcast, based upon their tokens dildo will start vibrate and the broadcaster will not be in control. Broadcaster will do anything to the user based upon their tokens.

After knowing these he was really eager and not willing to waste much time, his body temperature was pretty much high. At the home page there is an option called "BROADCAST YOURSELF". After clicking, there comes another small screen on the left "START BROADCASTING". This was his first broadcast and he wanted to check his webcam quality. He opened his webcam shutter on top of his screen.

VII

His webcam was not clear as HD and the broadcasting screen was small so he adjusted the monitor webcam to focus his face. Right of the broadcast screen there is chat screen to speak with users. On top of the chat screen there are 2 tabs says "Home and No: of Users". In home screen profile bio will appear in the brown text. Whenever the broadcaster change their bio automatically the updated bio will appear in the home screen. In the second tab there will be the users name joined to the room. If the user is the premium member then their name will be displayed in violet, non-premium member then the user name will be displayed in black and the broadcaster name will be in red.

He was just sitting and looking at the screen and the webcam no one joined his room. He decided to look into other broadcaster room. There were thousands of room and he started one by one. Top broadcasters with thousands of users in their room were nude with dildo between their legs with music in their room. He marked few of the users as favourites and those users will be displayed in his profile. There were screens now he was doing ALT + TAB to change the screens quickly. There were no users in his room till now, it's been 20 minutes of broadcasting. He realised that only women's can join his room and it takes time. He again waited someone to join in his room and he done ALT + TAB and changed his screen. He got horny and now he literally wanted someone to have a chat. He again changed the screen and clicked on the 2 tab (No: of users) the screen got refreshed, now id name kavya_789 joined his room.

He got a message in his home screen now the screen says "Home (1)" and the tab got highlighted in orange. He clicked on the home tab and now the user has messaged him.

Kavya_789: Hi PM

He did not understand what she is telling. This is the first time he is experiencing it. He continued his chat.

Mobby007: Hi ...what is pm?

Kavya_789: Private message.

Mobby007: How to do that?

Kavya_789: Right click and u will see the option.

He right clicked and he did not get any option as pm. He was nervous that he should not miss her.

Mobby007: I done but I did not get the option.

Kavya_789: Right click on the id.

He right clicked on her id and finally he got few options like "Message, Profile, Silence, Kick, Ban, and Promote to moderator". He clicked on message option and sent Hi to her. She replied within seconds

Kavya_789: Finally u found.

Mobby007: Yeah. U from?

Kavya_789: India and u?

Mobby007: Same here...state?

Kavya_789: TN.

His energy got raised when coming to know that she is tamilian. There was a smile in his face. He did not ask any more info about her. He got satisfied by knowing that she is tamilian.

Mobby007: Single?

She replied yes.

Mobby007: Name?

Kavya_789: Kavya and u?

He did not reply his name and he was not serious about the relationship, he just wanted someone to be always speaking with him like a partner. Always be there for him.

Mobby007: R u alone r with parents?

Kavya_789: Staying with parents...but now I'm alone.

Mobby007: Can u follow me?

He was not sure whether she will follow him.

Kavya_789: Done.

He came to know that users will do anything to make broadcaster happy and now she followed him, his first follower.

Mobby007: R u studying r working?

Kavya_789: Studying in Chennai...u?

Again he did not answer her question, everything was secret.

Mobby007: I'm here only for timepass and chat..nothing serious.

Kavya_789: I asked few questions to u but ur not replying anything to me and keep on asking questions.

Mobby_789: What u want to know tell me.

Now his message did not deliver to the user and she left his room and the chat window says" User Kavya_789 is no longer available in the room."

He got disappointed, now he learned that he wanted to keep his users engaged and he wanted to turn the users on to maintain the chat and keep his users available in his room for long time. This was his first experience and he wanted this badly to find a naughty and a horny partner. Now he checked the clock, it was 6PM and he stopped the broadcast, closed all the browsers and made the system to shut down.

VIII

He logged in back again to the system and he checked his outlook calender. Every Mondays, Tuesdays, Wednesdays he has client calls at 6:30PM. He partially completed his work and got up and went to terrace again and opened Instagram again, she is still active. He was wondering whether she is mobile addict or chatting with someone. Again he started texting her

"U have a boyfriend now r single?". Then he got an unexpected reply.

"Broke up recently". She had a relationship before and she is not virgin.

"I never had a relationship with anyone..I'm even looking for someone"

"Bad luck"

"Bad luck?" and there are two emoji's "You know what...

I'm not looking at

them ...know the difference first"

"Oh"

"What u do by the way...working?"

"Yeah...why you are enquiring in detail?"

"I need to know about you right...I'm not speaking with u only for sex"

"All boys say same things."

"I'm different and there is another smiling emoji."

"N see there is nothing to be shameful about if u like sex..It's fine dear."

"I'm being honest babe...even I'm not shameful."

"Okay...I hope you are speaking truth."

"Believe and trust me. I will be with u after this virus leaves. If not u can curse me."

"So u mean u love me?"

"Absolutely"

"Really?"

"Without looking at each other."

"okay.Then can u help me?"

.

"What."

.

"I need money"

.

He got a doubt on her whether she is trying to cheat him by getting the money. He did not reply anything for few minutes. He started to think about his work, family and expenses. He is the only source of income to his family. Entire family is depending upon him now in this pandemic situation. Even if she is asking small amount he decided not to give her money. Now his inner voice started to speak with him.

"You are working like a slave and you are earning. You doesn't know her personally and neither she is. Are you going to afford your money to a stranger? No". He started to think few minutes before speaking with her." What if she got the expected money and cheat on me? Now if I give her the money what she wanted and what if she started to blackmail me saying that, I have your chats I will go to police by saying I'm calling her to have sex."

Then he looked in to their chats he saw 3 dots floating which means she is typing something. Now the message came...

.

"Dear u want sex not relationship."

.

"What...how u can be so confident about that?"

.

"Yeah..if u want relationship then you would have asked for a casual meet

.

If ur interested in sex we could think of a casual hook-up and leave each other
after that."

.

He is really confused now whether he need sex or be in love with her without looking at her.

.

"Willing to share your watsapp number we can speak in watsapp?

.

Whatsapp? No not for now.

.

No calls, no pics , no videocalls, just chatting tats all.

.

I can send pics here and we can chat here as well. Number sharing is too fast.

.

U r free to go and look for someone else.

.

He is shocked now. She is not interested with him now but he need her no matter what. He did not leave her and not willing to. He started to type again and sent more messages.

.

Ok you said no whatsapp right? I did not see tat

.

Sry really sry

.

Fine?

.

Then she replied ok to him.

.

I will not ask pics and number till we meet...fine?cool?

There is no reply but she saw his messages. Again he started to text her.

Are u angry with me?

No reply again. Then texted back again to her by saying "Babbbyyyyyyy". No reply again.

Baby I said I'm sorry.

Then there is a heart below his message, she liked it but no reply again. He continuously sending messages to her and she is not replying back to him but seeing all his messages.

I mean it...please reply
See now only u started fighting and all.

Then finally her reply came by saying "Okay" to him. He replied her back " What do u mean by that."

"I'm not fighting".

From 6:30 I will be busy

In which company are you working?

MNC
He did not understand what she is trying to say.

MNC in which location?

What r u gng to get by knowing the location?

If it's near, I can come to meet you.

If u really love me then distance shouldn't matter.

Then she sent two sad emoji's. He came to know that she is still upset with him and now he wanted to make her smile.

Really? Still upset with me?

No. It's fine.

Ok wat should I do now to make u smile..you tell me I will do now

Don't do anything

Oh sure?

Finish your work then we'll talk about it.

Really?

Then shall I go with your permission madam.

Okay.

He knows she is angry on him and he is not willing to disturb her and he went offline.

IX

His phone battery was 15%. He plugged the charger and kept his phone on silent and kept charging till the call gets over. After the client call got over his phone battery was 45%. He decided to keep his phone charging until the battery reaches more than 95%. He was using MI A3 model which is quite quick in charging. His mom woke up before his call and working in kitchen preparing tea and they have a few plain cakes and chips for snacks. His mom has spinal cord disc problem at the position L4 & L5. She wears a belt around her hip due to this problem. She got this price when she was taking care of her mother in law. This was during his college time. Raju's sister-in-law Santhi. She is irresponsible when it comes to family. She doesn't take care of anyone. She is always money minded women. Due to her activities no one in the family except her husband likes her. Everyone in the village know about her character and what type of women she is. When Raju and his family moved to Hosur, Devi should be taken care by Santhi, because of her carelessness, Devi got stroke and all the family members decided to shift Devi from village to Hosur.

Devi was 95+ years old when she came to Hosur. Poornima was the one who took care of her during that time. She is the one and only women who left her husband for 8 yrs and stayed in village just to take care of Devi and got her first price from an asshole guy and moved out from village. Now again Devi re-entered into her life with stroke. She took care of her for more than 2 yrs by caring her from bed to bathroom and cleaning her bed, washing her clothes, feeding her, putting diapers for her motion leakage and she got her second price, disc problem. Sharan always felt proud of his mother, wherever she is, there is always respect for her. Entire family know the difference between Santhi and his mother and everybody know who is more responsible when it comes to family.

After their snacks time, his mom done Pooja and sat near him in the sofa.

Sharan asked "What did you pray mom?"

"I did not pray anything" said Poornima.

"Then?" asked Sharan.

"I said thanks" she said.

"What?"

"Yes. In this situation everyone most of the employees lost their jobs, no money, no food, few left houses and working somewhere outside the state those where trapped not able to travel to their hometown to see their family due to this lockdown. We are safe here and we have income from you and from dad. We have food, shelter and the most important thing is, we 3 are together and now you are working from home. We 3 are before gods eyes and we are one of the gifted family only god is with us in this situation. That's the reason I said thanks to god instead of praying. We should always thank god for what he has given to us and learn to be happy with what we are having instead of praying and asking more from him".

"Thank you for your advice mom" said Sharan and laughed.

She tapped on his arms and asked "How is work going on?"

"Same work mom no changes really boring" said Sharan like he is no longer interested in work anymore.

His mom turned his ears and said "Just now I said we are gifted try to perform well and get the promotion this time."

"Don't remember me that mom"

She smiled and said "Prepare and do well."

This was before lockdown, Sharan is quick learner and he is capable of thinking out of the box but, he always take second chance from the day one he entered into the professional life. At the start of mentoring and during viva for the certification he did not clear the viva on the first attempt he took second chance. Now for the promotion interview, he prepared well but he did not perform during the interview and he lost the promotion. He felt really bad when he came out from the interview. In office when the employee got promotion all the managers will call the employee name in front of everyone and there will be whistle and applause for them. He was standing in the corner and leaning towards the wall and clapping for others. He was missing this moment badly but he did not feel jealous because this was his mistake. Again his mind voice is speaking now.

"This was your mistake, you did not perform well. You should have gone there, you should have shacked your hands with managers or boss. Everyone would have congratulated you but now everything is opposite. There is no use of feeling low now. There is always a second chance for everything but, there is no chance more than that. Prepare well and show your best like no one ever shown.

Your time starts now".

One thing he learned from his failures is, success or failures we will be the one who is 100% responsible, there is nothing to be blame someone our managers or boss. Instead of blaming others try to know where you are lagging and try to improve at that specific point. Success will be in front of you. Before he was broke, he survived. Now he know his weak, he prepared. This is his second chance for the promotion.

He went to his room and looked at his phone now battery is 100%. He decided not to chat with her again till the interview gets over. Now he started to prepare for his interview and took notes in a paper and started to stick on the wall near to the monitor. During his interview it will be helpful for him if he stuck in the middle of his answers. Company didn't provide laptop due to sudden lockdown and WFH. He was having desktop during his interview and it doesn't support video call option. He knew that even if he look into his notes during the interview no one will come to know. His mom came inside to clean the room and saw his notes and smiled and asked

"What are you doing?" she asked.

"Cheating mom" he said.

"What cheating?" she asked in a confused manner.

"These are my notes for the interview. If I forgot or stuck in the middle of the answers these notes will be helpful" he said.

"What if they come to know that you are cheating?" Poornima asked.

"This does not support the video call option mom, only audio. They will never come to know" he said in a confident way.

There were 6 papers stacked on the wall, near to the monitor and he was looking at the papers like an investigator in the crime scenes.

He sat and looking into his mentoring notes for a complete revision and now he logged in again into his system and accepted his meeting invite for his interview.

"Dear come lets have dinner" said his mom.

"2 minutes mom" he said.

He locked his system, switched off the lights and stood before the mirror near the dressing table. One thing he know for sure he was broke like hell before, now he bounced back no one can stop him from his promotion.

XI

Sun rays inside his room and now he woke up. This is the day which he was waiting for, this is the day which he was looking for. Now he switched on the mobile data and there was no messages from her.

He said good morning and no reply from her for few minutes and texted again..

.

Baby I'm back

.

She liked his messages whenever he call her as baby.

.

Hey..beauty what you are doing

.

Nothing

.

Is anyone near you?

.

She did not reply for a minute

.

Can you reply me fast?

.

No one

.

Can I come?

.

Nooo

.

I'm the one who always should be near you

.

Why?

.

Husband only should be near right?

.

Yeah..you are not my husband

.

Really?

.

Yeah I'm not your husband...future husband

.

Future husband?

.

yes

.

Hmm

.

Are you sitting or sleeping somewhere else

.

Sitting

.

U told I'm only for sex right? So I need sex and ..sex only
with u.

.

Hmm.

.

Babe can I have your pic...I will send mine.

Not now

.

After some time

.

Some time?

.

10- 10:30

.

After dinner

.

you and your friends will be cooking for dinner r u guys order
Cooking
Oh kk...what are all the dishes you know to cook...favourite dish.
Why??
Normal roti sabji

.

How many dishes you know to cook

.

Why??
I know all the basic dishes.

.

Then no problem for me

.

Ok

.

What else? How s work? Are you doing wfh?

.

Yeah

.

How s work?

Good
Tell me about you
Wat u do?

.

I'm working

.

Where?
He used her trick and told 'MNC' she replied back to him as 'Clever'.
So tell me what would u prefer a date with me or a one night stand?

.

U r interested only in one night stand?

.

I have lost belief in long term relationship

.

K thn..lets meet each other...I will spend one day with u thn we can go to ur flat...evng we can go to ur room only me and u..thn everything continues in a flow...we can be in touch for few months r yrs...if u trust me with ur heart and soul thn we can move to relationship.
Ok
See I'll tell you my thoughts.

.

Ok.

.

If I think that a boy is of my type then I will spend some time with him
B4 having any physical relationship.
N I feel someone isn't of my type thn just a casual hookup and end all.

.

Hookup like just meet, speak and gng?

She liked his message now. He came to know that she doesn't like sex. Then he got a satisfied reply.

Only sex.

Now he is satisfied, today he is going to rock in his interview. With smiling face, he got out from his bed took his trimmer and got trim, he need to look good during his interview and had a warm shower.

Had his breakfast and he switched off his mobile, now is reading time. He started to read NYPD 1st part series by his favourite author James Patterson.

Now time is 2:30PM had his lunch and came to login at 3:00PM and looked at his notes for everything is perfect. He took his phone and switched back on and opened voice recording app. He started to practice his introduction and recorded it and he listened to his own voice. His voice and flow was not perfect not terrible, average. He did not leave his confidence, still he had time. His interview was 6:30-7:00PM. He was structuring his own voice. His confidence became much stronger when before when he heard his voice changeover and his continues flow of his introduction. He took a few minutes break he took a long breath before entering his room and he had few minutes for the moment which he was waiting for.

"Best of luck my dear son" and she kissed his cheek.

"Thank you mom" he said.

He opened his room door and entered into his room. He had last 10 mins for his interview to start.

He logged in into his system and there was a message from someone his manager told him best of luck he did not reply instead he started his interview meeting. He joined first then after a couple of minutes everyone joined the meeting and his time had started. Meeting started with greetings and with his structured voice he completed his introduction and he got a compliment from his manager for his introduction. Then continued with the process questions and he answered most of them correctly by his notes and few he missed. Overall his performance was satisfactory and far better than his previous interview. He disconnected the call, locked his system, took a long breath and opened his door, his mom switched off the lights and television in the hall. She was sitting on the stool near to his room door and she was hearing from the start to end of his interview.

"Mom, what you are doing?" he asked.

"I was listening to you. How it went?" she asked.

"Very well mom. Much better than previous time, answered most of the questions and few I got confused started to blabber something. Nice mom, it was nice" he said in a satisfied manner.

"Nice to hear this from you. You were so stressed and you felt so bad after the first attempt. This is how should be, always learn from failures and should bounce back not only in interviews even in your life" she said.

"Mom, I need some water not advice. My throat got dried" he said.

She smiled and gave him a lime juice instead of water.

"When did you prepare this?" he asked.

"Before your interview got started" she said in a smiling face.

Both went to terrace had a fresh air and walked for half an hour and now both are satisfied. They came down and during their dinner he told the entire story to his father. After dinner he went to this room and logged in his system now time is 10:30PM. H took his phone and opened Instagram and she is stil active. In this joyful moment he eagerly waiting to see her pic. He started tying now.

.

                              Just completed dinner...wbu?

                                                    .

Done.

.

                                             Cool..pic?

                                                    .

Yaa...I forgot abt that

.

                                        One s enough

                                                    .

Okay

.

She sent it. His fingers were shaking and he clicked on blue "Photo" icon. He saw her. She was wearing pink saree. He was not able to guess her height because she was in a sitting posture one hand on her knees and the other hand were on her chubby cheeks, free hair, and fair skin. She was in little makeup in that picture. He doesn't want to take eyes from that pic and he badly want this pic. He took screenshot of her pic and save in his phone. This day will be his one of his memorable day. Got satisfied from his interview and now he saw her pic and there was a text from her.
Happy?
He said yes and sent few love emoji's to her.

.

You took screenshot? She asked.

.

He got shocked how she came to know, may be Instagram sent notification to her based on the privacy policies. He doesn't want to lie her so he said the truth.

.

Ya...do u want to delete?

Wen we r meeting I will be able to recognise u..tats y

It's ok...u can keep.

U liked it?

U r awesome and chubby

Ya I'm chubby but not fat

Tats wat I needed

Why chubby?

Chubbies will be good, everything will be pretty much bigger

Hmm

Wat u had for dinner?

Nothing special

U did not tell me ur area...thn how we r gng to meet

When we meet I'll tell you

Sure...I think instead of pink black suits u...it's my favourite colour

Hmm..ya...transparent black saree, sleeve and less blouses

Even I do like transparent saree only wen ur with me

Hmm

U wore those to ur office also?

No..only in parties.

He sent 2 crying emoji's and she asked what happened, he replied in a jealous "Then everybody would have seen those?

She is sure what he mentioned as those. She is clever in THOSE and she liked his message. Now time its 12:00 AM his shift time is going to end in another half an hour. He checked his mails and completed all his work and logged out.

XIII

Only for her studies and work she left her hometown and her family. During her college she stayed in hostel and she have been living together for few years and single now. She is Marathi. Those pics she sent on yesterday was taken before, she laid with Rahul. He was her college senior during exams she sat near to him. Both are in the same department and by sitting near to each other they had more conversations and exchanged their numbers even their bed. Her parents doesn't know about her life. She believed and trusted next to her parents. He was completely opposite to her. He is working in a start-up company and his boss is a psycho. He always get stressed due to his work and his boss. She is a stress buster. He always wanted to get laid with her like, use and throw paper. This pity girl doesn't know who actually he is. She gave her heart and soul to him but she got nothing only betrayal.

On 23rd Jul was his birthday both were in their room and arranging for his birthday party. He was taking shower. His phone rang

"Baby someone is calling you dear" she said

"Keep in silent. I will be back in few minutes" he said.

There were 43 messages, few were birthday messages to him and few were images and that was not downloaded. She clicked on the downloading option. Her eyes got wider, her hands started shaking, sweat was flowing down on her temple, her vision got blur and tear started to fell on his phone display. Those were not birthday messages, sex chats, images and audios. She came to know that he has created a fake dating website and dating more than 5 girls including her simultaneously. He has sent her pictures and had recorded their sex video. She has no idea what is going on in her life. Everything he told to her was a lie. Each and every word was a lie, each and every minute, each and every second was a lie and betrayal. She was not able to tolerate her betrayal. She heard his sound next to her. She wiped his tear and stood at the same place by controlling her tears.

He hugged her from back and he moved his hands upon her belly and kissed on her right shoulder.

"Babe are you ready for tonight?" he said by kissing her.

She closed her eyes and kept his phone inside her pocket. He doesn't know that she has another plan for him tonight. She turned and looked at him and pushed him towards the bed on the right and said

"Yeah baby I'm ready. Get ready to see the real party tonight".

XIV

Entire room was decorated with balloons, ribbons and they switched off every lights only candles were lighted. Speakers were connected to his phone and there was a romantic piano music was playing in their room, both were holding their hands together and started dancing. He did not take his eyes from her. His right hand was holding her hand and his left hand was on her back. She was opposite to him. Full of anger her eyes were red and she was holding her emotions from very long time. It's like ice versus fire. He started to kiss her on forehead, nose and turned her. There was no love, no trust in him. She was standing ideally without any movements. He removed his shirt and pants. He was horny and when he was trying to undress her, there was a notification sound from one of their phones. He was completely forgot about his phone. She started smiling now. He left her and started searching his phone. He searched his shirt and pant pockets everything was empty. Then suddenly he realized that he was telling her to keep his phone in silent when he was in shower. He looked at her, there she was raising his phone up, now she is looking at him and raised the music volume.

"What you are doing with my phone?" he asked.

She did not reply. Looking at him for a few seconds. She kept her first step towards him. Her hair was not combed and few were touching her eyes. She was like a murderer.

"You lied to me" she said in full of anger.

"What?" he said in low voice.

"You betrayed me" her tears started to flow.

"Uhhh…Babe" he said.

"Don't ever call me that again" she shouted and throwed his phone. It bounced and hits his face. When he looked his phone was unlocked.

"Phone was not locked when you got the call from Alexandra" she said.

"How you know Alexandra?" he said.

"I know each and everything about you, Alexandra, your clients and about your website" she said.

"Web…" he was speechless when she mentioned about website.

"How you know all these?" he stood up now.

She took the birthday knife which was before her and said "Bastard, do you know the meaning of love?" she said by looking at the knife in her hand and she was coming close to him.

"Do you know what love is and you have no idea know how it hurts when you trust someone with your soul and got betrayal back" she said and started to run towards him. He was running to get his gun in the next room. She throwed the knife to his left ankle and he was on the ground. Begging her to keep him alive. She dragged him to the hall and the blood strains were on the floor. She took the other knife, from the knife stand which was on the dining table. She sat upon him and said

"How's the party baby?" laughed and punched his nose till she saw his blood. She removed the knife from his ankle very hard .He was crying and screaming in pain. She was out of control and no one to help him.

"Shhhhh..." she stood up and closed the front door and locked it.

"Do you think women's are sex toys to you?" she asked and there was a laptop bag near to the sofa. She went to look at his bag and he took her leg. She turned and kicked his balls.

"No please don't touch that" his voice was breaking in pain.

She opened the bag there were pistols, masks and a laptop. She took the laptop and pressed enter, it was locked. He started to laugh and she kicked his balls again.

"Are you going to tell me the password or..." before she completes it, there was a skype call and she turned and smiled at him.

"Who was that? Who was that? Tell me bitch!!!" he said in anger.

"Ok.ok...whoever maybe please don't accept it. Did you understand?" he said.

"No. I did not understand" she said and attended the call. It was a video call, before pressing the enter she switched off the video from her end. She was mid-thirties with long brown hair, blue eyes and should be Latin American. Her guessing was correct she is Alexandra.

"Switch on the video?" she said. Her voice was in high pitch with Greek accent.

She decided to speak with her in the chat and started typing in the chat box.

"Some issues with my laptop..I'm not able to switch it on and audio is not working" and clicked on SEND.

"Ok, whatever. Listen to me carefully. I need 2 of them before next week is it possible?" she said.

She typed "Yes" and sent.

"Great. There is a conference on next week in our headquarters and bring those 2 girls directly to our conference" she said in a low voice. She started typing now.

"I don't think I will make to conference" she sent.

"WTF..Are you mad? Everyone are waiting for this conference to be conducted. Any reason?" she got tensed.

"I'm not gonna be alive tonight" she typed and sent to Alexandra.

"What are you saying..are you drunk?" she asked.

Now she switched on the video camera. There he is, on the floor. Both his legs and hands were tied in rope. He was sweating, his face was damaged and at back of him she saw someone with joker mask with knife. She dragged him close to the camera and kept the knife in his throat.

"No...wait..who..who are you, what do you want?" she got frightened.

"Do you think women's are slaves and toys for you?" she asked her.

"Ok..what do you want now? How much money you need?" she asked.

She laughed and inserted the knife into the both sides of his neck. He was screaming loud then she removed the knife from neck and punched the knife into his mouth. Blood spilled everywhere on the floor. She came close to the camera and said

"No need money. I need you. I'm coming for you. Stop me if you can".

XV

Sunrays inside her room, she woke up and she saw fan in the roof. It was all dream. The dream which shouldn't come again in her life. The dream which she want to forget. Her love, her betrayal, her trust everything she want to get rid of it. She want her mind to be free so she started looking for someone who cares and someone who wants to listen her past and her dreams. She selected Instagram and now her new friend in Instagram doesn't know all of her past and her first murder. She doesn't want to tell her past to anyone until she feel comfortable, secure and more trustable with someone. She got up from bed, made her breakfast and sat on sofa. It's been more than 2 years now after her murder no one from police department, CBI were able to find who performed this and what was the intention of this murder. She doesn't care about any police or CBI. She was only focused on Alexandra and her clients. Before killing her she wants to know what's the reason behind these fake websites and why she is targeting only women's. Her only thing in mind was to know, who all involved in this and she needs to kill of them and destroy this fake website. Now she has only one laptop, one phone and her new friend to do all this.

STORY IS NOT ENDED, IT'S JUST THE BEGINNING.